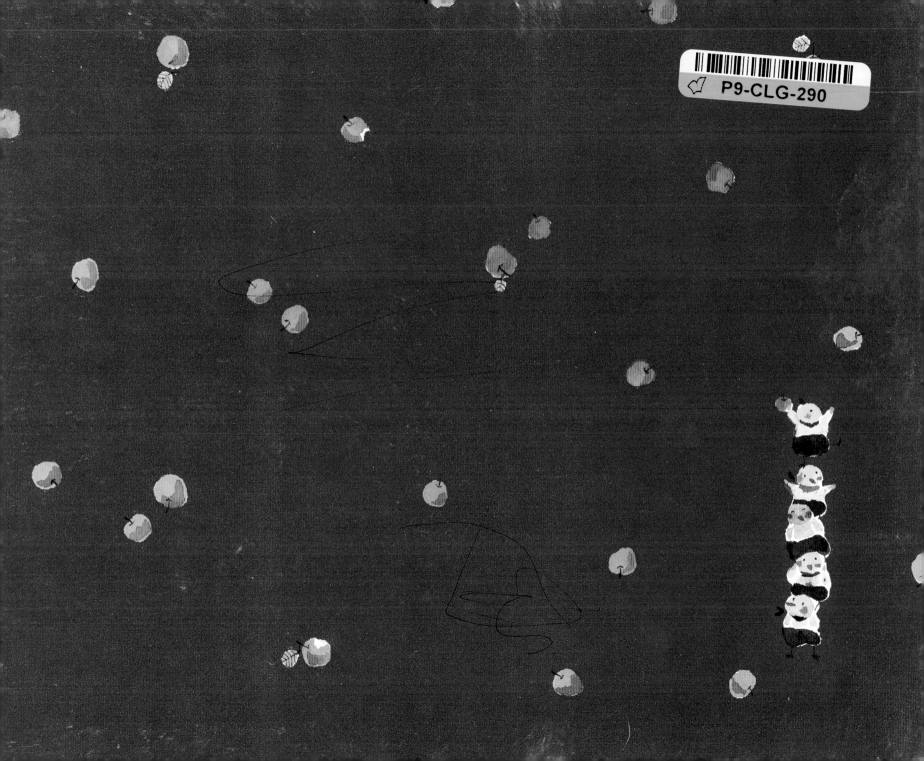

To Mrs. A-B: apples for a tip-top teacher—L. B.

To Koharu—H. N.

Henry Holt and Company, LLC
Publishers since 1866
175 Fifth Avenue
New York, New York 10010
www.HenryHoltKids.com

Library of Congress Cataloging-in-Publication Data
Berry, Lynne.
Ducking for apples / Lynne Berry ; illustrated by Hiroe Nakata. — 1st ed.
p.   cm.
Summary: Five little ducks ride bicycles and gather apples to make a sweet treat.
ISBN 978-0-8050-8935-6
[1. Stories in rhyme. 2. Ducks—Fiction. 3. Bicycles and bicycling—Fiction. 4. Apples—Fiction.]
I. Nakata, Hiroe, ill. II. Title.
PZ8.3.B4593Dun 2010   [E]—dc22   2009027412
First Edition—2010
The artist used watercolor and ink to create the illustrations in this book.
Printed in May 2010 in China by South China Printing Company Ltd., Dongguan City,
Guangdong Province, on acid-free paper. ∞

1 3 5 7 9 10 8 6 4 2

Ducking for Apples

Lynne Berry

ILLUSTRATED BY Hiroe Nakata

HENRY HOLT AND COMPANY ● NEW YORK

"Blue sky! Sunshine! Head outside!
Let's ride bikes!" five ducks decide.
"Training wheels?" the first two say.
Three little ducklings shout, "No way!"

Five bold ducks
on ten thin wheels
Wobble, bobble,
squeak, and squeal.

One duck teeters.

Two ducks swerve.

Three ducks totter.

Four ducks curve.

Five little ducks now ride full-steam.
"Can't catch us—we're the great duck team!"

Five ducks, slowing, climb a hill.
Huff-puff! Huff-puff! Huff until . . .

. . . Five ducks reaching for the sky
Soar downhill as the wind whips by.

Wind-swept ducklings coast to a stop
At a rock by a tree with a snack on top.
"Yippee! Apples!" two ducks call.
"Stack up, stack up, five ducks tall!"

One little duck at the top of the stack
Reaches tiptoe for the snack.
One little duckling, still so high,
Picks more apples for a pie,

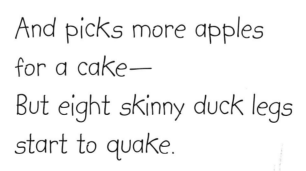

And picks more apples
for a cake—
But eight skinny duck legs
start to quake.

"Hurry! Hurry!" four ducks shout.
Too late! Duck legs all give out.

Duck stack crumbles. Apples tumble.
"I'm still *hungry*," four ducks grumble.

One little duck says, "Scoot around!
Gather apples from the ground!"

Ducks scoop apples. Oops! Some spill.

Ducks walk bikes back up the hill.

Ducks zip homeward, coast, and brake,

Tramp inside, and start to bake.

Three little ducks cut fruit in slices,
Mix with sugar, toss with spices.
Two little ducks press sticky dough
Down in the dish where the fruit will go.

Ducklings bake their apple treat,

Top with whipped cream: "Eat, ducks, eat!"

Five ducks lick five sticky beaks,
Sticky fingers, sticky cheeks.
And full of pie and full of cream,
Ducks drift off to a sweet duck dream.

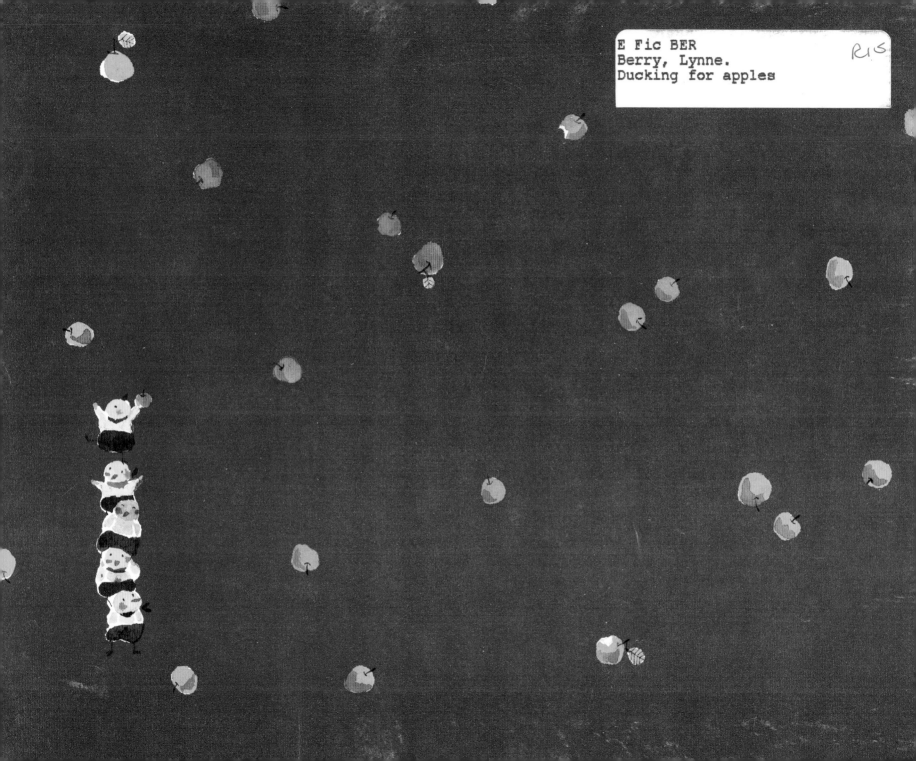